Mumba Tales: Mumba Monkey and the Spider

By Deborah Orr

Mumba's Vocabulary Words

1. **Camouflage**-An animals natural coloring or form that enables it to blend in with its surroundings.

2. **Chrysalis**-(Sometimes called a cocoon.) The hard-shelled pupa of a moth or butterfly.

3. **Hesitated**-To think twice before doing something.

4. **Language**-The ways in which humans communicate.

5. **Merriment**-To have fun.

6. **Rainforest**-A rainforest is a forest that receives heavy rainfall.

Dedicated
To My
Children, grandchildren, nephews, nieces and
all the creative children in the world.

JFALI Press

Published as an e-book

ISBN # 978-0-9793878-4-5

Long ago, there was a magical rain forest. The magic came from the rain. After it rained long and hard for couple of days, strange things would happen. Some of the changes were scary, like snakes being able to walk and run, and monkeys being able to speak and read the language of man.

The creatures of the forest said it was the work of Nyme, the great sky God who controlled the rains. One of the smallest creatures in the magic forest was Spider. Although he was small, he was very mean, and he hated the chattering of the monkeys and other creatures. When the next big rain came, he was in a deep, dark mood, and stayed out in the forest, shouting and fussing. When the raindrops started falling hard and fast, Spider passed out.

When the spider finally opened his eyes, he didn't quite feel like himself. As He pulled himself up from the ground, he happened to look toward the pond —and he couldn't believe what he saw looking back at him.

He recognized his face, he was huge. In fact, he was as big as an orangutan. Spider laughed so hard; he got the attention of the other creatures. The monkeys were shocked, and soon their chatter filled the forest. The mean little spider was now a big, mean spider.

Spider decided to set some traps to help him find the one monkey who really made him angry, because he was always bragging about reading and making merriment. The monkey's name was Mumba Monkey.

One day the monkey fell asleep near one of the traps Spider had set, and Spider caught him.

Mumba Monkey, so rudely awakened from his nap, was scared!

"I know you don't want to eat me, oh great Spider, for I'm just an ugly old monkey. If you want a wonderful treat, you need to capture the most beautiful thing in the forest."

11

"And what is the most beautiful thing in the forest?" Spider asked.

"It's the caterpillar, Spider. One day, after the caterpillar has eaten up almost everything, she will become something beautiful and fly away. You need to hurry and find her before that happens," said Mumba Monkey.

"What will she become?" asked Spider.

"You don't know what she will become?" Mumba Monkey asked slyly. "Don't you read?"

"I hate that word, read! I don't need to read," Spider replied, getting angry.

"Well, it's one way to find out about things," Mumba Monkey said.

"I'm getting hungry, Mumba Monkey," warned Spider.

"Spider, don't you want to become the most beautiful thing in the whole rain forest, and fly to the heavens? If you eat Caterpillar, that is what will happen!" Mumba Monkey was getting worried.

"Well, I guess I do," said Spider. "You may go, monkey, but don't tell the caterpillar that I'm looking for her."

Mumba Monkey was swinging through the trees when he looked down and saw Caterpillar below, eating a luscious, fat leaf. Mumba Monkey dropped down, starling the caterpillar.

"Oh, Mumba Monkey, it's only you! You scared me! Why are you in such a hurry?" asked Caterpillar.

"I have been looking for you, Caterpillar. Spider is looking for you, too. He wants you for dinner."

"Oh, I would love to come to dinner!" the caterpillar exclaimed. "What is he serving?"

"Caterpillar," replied Mumba Monkey.

"Did you just say Caterpillar?" asked Caterpillar, gulping.

"I'm afraid Spider wants to eat you for dinner, Caterpillar," Mumba Monkey answered.

"But why me, Mumba Monkey? I am no match for Spider. Besides, I am small, and now that he is so big, why would he want to eat such a tiny insect? How will I protect myself?" asked Caterpillar, worried.

"There must be something you can do," said Mumba Monkey.

Caterpillar thought very hard. Then she had an idea.

"Mumba Monkey, I know what I can do. When Spider comes after me, I will blend in with the leaves and flowers around me. It's called camouflage. If I look like my surroundings, he won't be able to see me."

"That's a good plan Caterpillar."

" How will I know when he's coming, Mumba Monkey?" asked Caterpillar.

"When the trees and leaves start moving, even if there's no wind. And all the monkeys will begin to call out to warn the creatures in the forest. When those things happen, you must hide!" said Mumba Monkey.

"Thank you for warning me, Mumba Monkey," said Caterpillar. You're a real friend. "

The monkey jumped back up into the tree and quickly swung, swung, swung out of sight. Suddenly, the leaves on the trees began swaying back and forth, even though there was no wind. The monkeys started swinging, swinging, swinging through the canopy, and began to chatter as if to warn Caterpillar.

She felt sure that Spider must be coming, so she moved into the thick of the trees and bushes,and blended right in with the dark green leaves.

When Spider reached the spot where Caterpillar has been, he couldn't find her anywhere.

Tired of waiting, Spider put a call out for Mumba Monkey. As soon as the monkey got the message, he came to see what Spider wanted.

"Mumba Monkey, why is it that I can never catch the caterpillar?" Spider asked. "Tell me, does she do magic and make herself disappear?"

"Oh, no," said Mumba Monkey. "What Caterpillar can do is called camouflage, but it's not magic. She can blend in with the leaves and flowers of the forest, and no one can find her."

"Well," huffed Spider, "maybe it's time for Mumba Monkey stew!"

"Oh, no," said Mumba Monkey. "I know how you can catch Caterpillar."

"How?" asked Spider.

"There is a leaf that she loves to eat. It is the leaf of the dewberry plant. Caterpillar loves this plant more than anything in the forest. Once she has tasted the leaf, she won't stop eating until she has eaten the last leaf from the plant. I will get the plant and bring it to you."

"Don't take too long," Spider warned.

Mumba Monkey searched through the rain forest until, at last, he found a dewberry plant. He pulled it up and hurried to give it to Spider.

"Here is a dewberry plant, Spider," said Mumba Monkey.

"Good work, Mumba Monkey.

As Mumba Monkey quickly disappeared, Spider took the dewberry plant to Caterpillar's feeding area and set a trap for her.

Several days later, Caterpillar went to her favorite spot. To her surprise, she saw a dewberry plant that had not been there before. She hesitated a moment, wondering how the plant had gotten there, but in spite of her suspicions, she couldn't stop herself from taking a bite of a tender leaf.

Once she had tasted the leaves, she had to have more, and kept cramming them into her mouth.

The caterpillar became so sleepy and full of the delicious plant, she couldn't move. Spider jumped up and pinned the caterpillar to the ground.

"I have finally captured you, Caterpillar!" Spider exclaimed.

"Oh, great Spider, I am just a little caterpillar. There are many other creatures in the forest that are larger and tastier than me, so why do you want to eat me?"

"Because Mumba Monkey told me you will become something very beautiful, and if I eat you, I will become something beautiful and fly away," said Spider.

"Mumba Monkey is my friend!" cried Caterpillar. "I don't believe you!"

"Mumba Monkey is not your friend," Spider laughed. "Mumba Monkey told me how to set a trap with the dewberry plant!"

"I guess Mumba Monkey is not my friend," said Caterpillar, hanging her head sadly.

"Now, tell me, what is it that you will you become, that can fly away?" asked Spider.

"I will attach myself to a branch of a tree. Then I will spin my chrysalis of the finest silk," Caterpillar said. "I cannot become this beautiful thing you want unless I can spin my chrysalis."

"The finest silk?Really?"asked Spider.

"Yes," said Caterpillar. "Then you will be the most beautiful thing that flies, wrapped in a coat of pure silk. Let me spin my chrysalis. After 10 days you must count to ten in English and Spanish, and then I will be ready to come out." Spider couldn't count, so he told the monkeys to count so he would know when to come back and get his coat of pure silk, which he could use to fly away.

After 10 days had passed, the monkeys high in the trees started counting:

One, two, three, four, five, six, seven, eight, nine, ten.

Uno, dos, tres, cuatro, cinco, seis, siete, ocho, nueve, diez.

Spider heard them, he was watching the trees.

Suddenly, the chrysalis burst wide open. Spider had often seen such beautiful creatures fluttering about in the rain forest, and now one flew directly above his head.

"Silly Spider, caterpillars turn into butterflies after they've eaten everything in their path."

"Wait! Come back here! Come back here right now!"

"Goodbye, Spider, I have to go visit all the beautiful flowers."

As Butterfly was flying away, she looked down and saw Mumba Monkey

"I should drop a mango on your head," said Butterfly.

"Who are you and what do you want?" asked Mumba Monkey.

"I was the caterpillar, and you told Spider how to catch me!" snapped Butterfly.

"Oh, Caterpillar, you have turned into a very beautiful butterfly," Mumba Monkey said. "I couldn't protect myself just moving from tree to tree, but I knew you would soon turn into a butterfly and fly away. I knew that you would outsmart Spider. I'm sorry, Butterfly. Will you still be my friend?"

"I forgive you, Mumba Monkey," Butterfly said. "I'm on my way to where the most beautiful flowers in the rain forest grow. Would you like to join me?"

"No, I'm going to stay here and stand up to Spider," said Mumba Monkey.

With that, Butterfly flew on her way. Mumba Monkey looked down and saw Spider coming, and Spider was very mad.

"Mumba Monkey, you tricked me! You knew all the time what the caterpillar would turn into," shouted Spider.

"So, Spider, you didn't know that caterpillars turn into butterflies? You better start reading," laughed Mumba Monkey.

With that , Mumba Monkey swung through the trees laughing , and all the monkeys in the trees began to chatter and sing

Spider, Spider crawls upon land
Trying to catch anything he can
He caught the caterpillar one fine day
Then she turned into a butterfly and flew away

Mumba Monkey threw his head back and laughed even louder: "Chee! Chee! Chee!"

"Be on guard, Mumba Monkey, because I'm going to get you one day soon!" Spider grumbled, crawling back toward his burrow.

[1]*Most people think caterpillars make a cocoon, but the correct term is chrysalis.*

Author Deborah L. Orr

debraorr89@yahoo.com

deborraut.com

Deborah Orr is a children's librarian, children's author, and playwright. She is originally from Detroit, MI, she graduated from **Wayne Community College, with an Associate of Arts, and received a Bachelor of Arts from Michigan State University. She holds a certificate from the University of Texas Library School in Children's Literature.**

She is dedicated to serving the community by providing puppetry, storytelling, reading and writing workshops to encourage learning. For the past twenty years she visited libraries in Georgia, Michigan and Texas, offering reading workshops. During the summers while staying in Detroit, she works closely with the summer reading club, sharing her stories and promoting reading at different libraries.

She is the author of **The Little Cornbread Girl, Mumba Tales, and Candice and the Beautiful Junk.** You can order her books as an e-book or paperback copy from Amazon. Ms. Orr also work closely with the non-profit organization, Outreach Productions, helping them promote reading.

The next story in the Mumba Tales series is, "Mumba and the Amazon Ants."

Illustrator-Ogbru Evidence

Ogbru Evidence is a multi-talented artist with over 8 years' experience in comic, book illustrations and figure drawing. He is well versed in the use of Adobe illustrator, sketchbook pro for illustrations as well as hand drawn illustrations. He brings you taste and excellence. You can contact him through fiverr.com under mlake_arts.

Editor-Anne Berry Daugherty

Anne Berry Daugherty, a graduate of Michigan State University, has been working as a freelance editor/copy editor for more than 22 years. Clients include DBusiness, Hour Detroit, and Detroit Home magazines; the Metropolitan Detroit Guest Guide and Metropolitan Detroit Dining Guide; and the Community Foundation for Southeast Michigan. She recently edited Detroit: Engine of America, a history of Detroit's first 200 years.

www.ingramcontent.com/pod-product-compliance
Lightning Source LLC
Chambersburg PA
CBHW041012170626
46815CB00003B/267